The Usborne

# OPTICAL ILLUSIONS
## Activity Book

Sam Taplin

Designed and illustrated by
**Stephanie Jones & Hanri Shaw**

Additional design by **Matt Durber & Kasia Dudziuk**

## CONTENTS

| | | | |
|---|---|---|---|
| 2-3 | What are optical illusions? | 20 | Colour confusion |
| 4-5 | Is it moving? | 21 | Baffling buildings |
| 6-7 | Tilting or straight? | 22-23 | Distorted shapes |
| 8 | How long are the lines? | 24-25 | Moving pictures |
| 9 | Is it the same size? | 26 | Magic circle |
| 10-11 | Crazy colours | 27 | Squashed shapes |
| 12-13 | Impossible dot-to-dots | 28-29 | Endless patterns |
| 14-15 | Ghostly pictures | 30 | Which way? |
| 16 | Bewildering spinners | 31 | Catch the bird |
| 17 | Imaginary shapes | 32 | Illusion puzzles |
| 18-19 | Can you follow the line? | | |

Colour the rest of the squares black, then move your eyes around the page.
Do you see dots appearing at the corners of the squares?

# What are optical illusions?

An optical illusion is an image that fools your eyes and makes you see something that isn't really there. In this book, you're going to make lots of amazing illusions by drawing, colouring and adding stickers to the pictures. Here are some of the different types of illusions you're going to create.

## CONFUSING COLOURS

Look at the two squares circled in red. They seem to be very different – one looks dark and the other pale. But amazingly, they're exactly the same colour. There are lots of extremely deceptive colour illusions like this, and you can make some of your own on pages 10 and 11.

## MOVING PICTURES

Stare at the middle block of squares, and move the book from side to side. Can you see the squares wobbling up and down? This is an example of a "movement" illusion, where a printed image seems to move in an impossible way. On pages 4 and 5 you can make your own versions.

# TILTING LINES

Do these lines appear to be tilting? In fact they're parallel, and it's only the pattern on the lines that confuses your eyes. It's easy to create illusions where straight lines seem bent, and you can try it yourself on pages 6 and 7.

# SHIFTING SHAPES

Which of these shapes seems largest? The pink one looks taller than the blue one – but in fact all four are identical. Many classic illusions are based on shapes, and you'll find some more on pages 22 and 23.

## WHAT YOU'LL NEED

To create most of the illusions all you'll need is a pen and the stickers at the back of the book. But you'll also need a few other things for some of the illusions. Here's a list:

- A thin black pen   • A thick black pen   • A ruler   • A drawing pin   • Sheets of paper   • Scissors
- Colouring pencils or pens   • A drinking straw   • Cocktail sticks   • A mug   • String   • A hole punch

# HOW TO USE THIS BOOK

It's important that you follow the instructions carefully, or the illusions might not work. Make sure you put the stickers in the right place, and when you have to draw or colour, do it neatly. You might want to photocopy some pages, so you can try again if you get it wrong.

Most optical illusions work well for most people, but not everyone can see every illusion. Some of these images will be more effective for your eyes than others, and you may find that a few don't seem to work at all. If this happens, just try the next one.

# Is it moving?

Usually it's only in stories that pictures come to life and start to move. But you're going to see all of the images on these pages move mysteriously right before your eyes.

ROTATING ARROWS

Find sticker 4 and stick it over the top of this circle.

Now move your eyes around the arrows. What happens?

# SPINNING CIRCLES

What happens to the circles on the right while you're reading this? Can you see them spin a little?

Find all the 5a stickers and add them in the blue spaces.

Now move your eyes around the circles. Are they spinning more now?

Notice how the circle you're looking directly at never spins – but the others do.

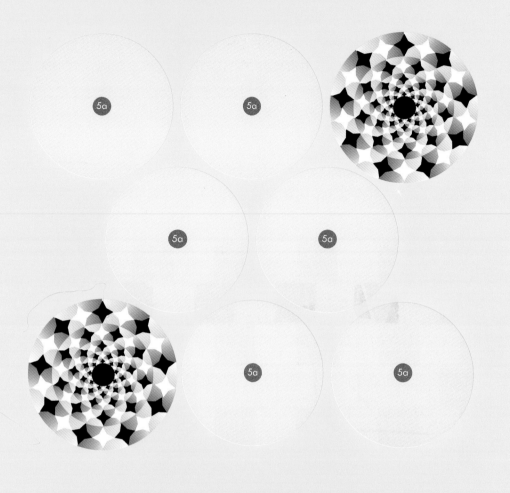

# UP AND DOWN

Find the 5b stickers and use them to complete the image on the right. Make sure both sets of arrows are pointing down.

Now move your eyes back and forth across the whole image. Can you see the arrows moving?

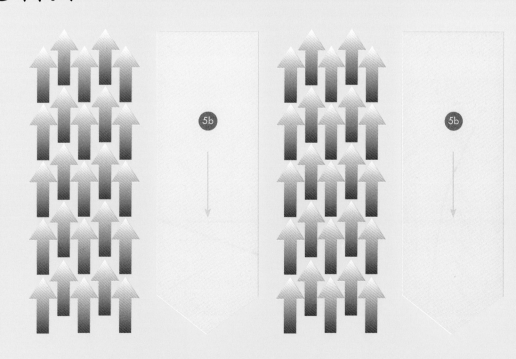

# Tilting or straight?

It should be easy to tell when lines are parallel, but illusions can make lines look so strange that you'll really believe they're tilting. On these pages, you're going to make that happen.

## WOBBLY WALL

Carefully colour the grey blocks in this pattern black. Now look at the pattern.

The horizontal lines are all parallel. But do they look it?

## LEANING LINES

The orange lines below are parallel, but the black lines make them seem tilted.

Draw in the rest of the black lines. Do all the vertical lines seem to tilt now?

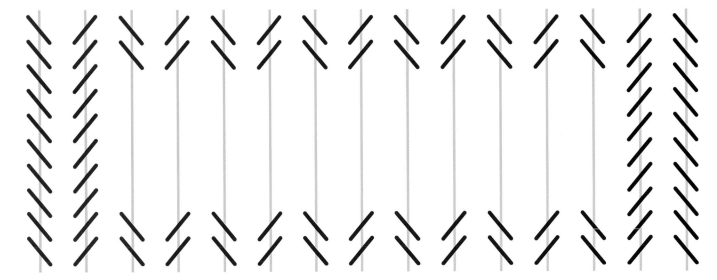

# PUZZLING PATTERNS

Using a ruler and a thin black pen, draw four horizontal lines onto the patterns below, between the pairs of red dots.

All the lines you've drawn are parallel. But if you move your eyes around the image they will seem to slant.

# BENDY BRIDGE

The white columns holding up this bridge are parallel, but soon they won't look it.

Draw in the missing slanting lines on each column. Can you see them tilting now?

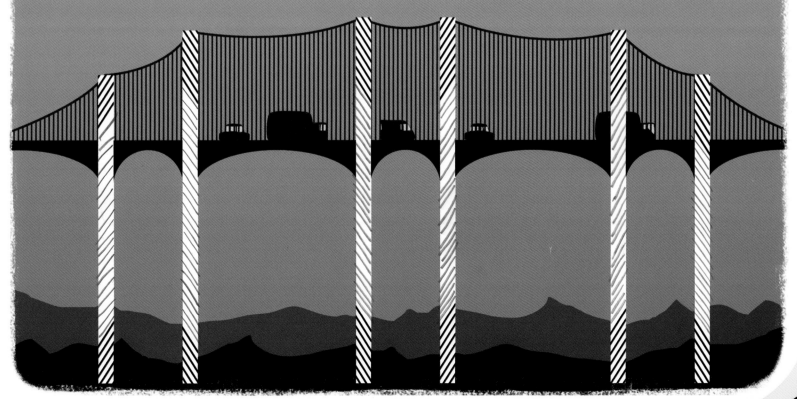

# How long are the lines?

How can two lines that are exactly the same length be made to look different? On this page, you're going to find out.

Using a ruler, draw a line between the two "A" dots on the right. Now draw a line between the two "B" dots. The two lines are the same length... but does one look longer?

Try the same thing with the other pairs of dots.

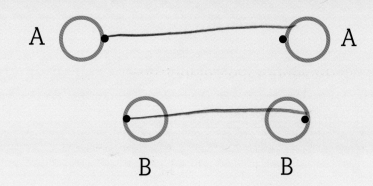

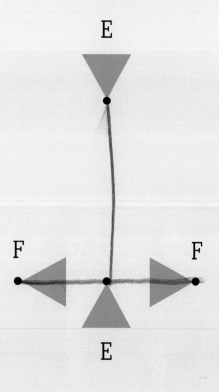

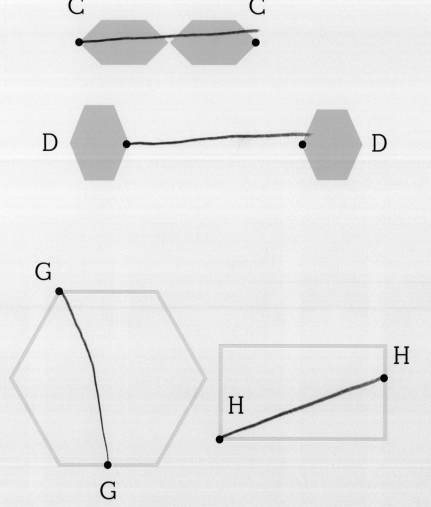

All the lines you've drawn on this page may look different — but in fact each one is the same length. Check them with a ruler.

# Is it the same size?

The way you judge the size of an object is affected by what's around it. You can explore this idea with the illusions below, where you'll make identical shapes seem different from each other.

Using a thin black pen and a ruler, draw over the dotted lines. Does one yellow square look bigger now?

Draw over these dotted lines with a thin black pen. Does one of the green circles look bigger now?

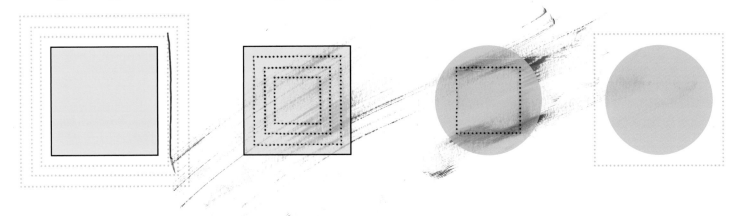

Add the 9a and 9b stickers around these circles, using the dots as a guide. Does one pink circle look bigger now?

Find the 9c stickers, which are the same size, and stick one in each circle. Do the stickers seem to be different sizes now?

Put the small 9a stickers around this circle.

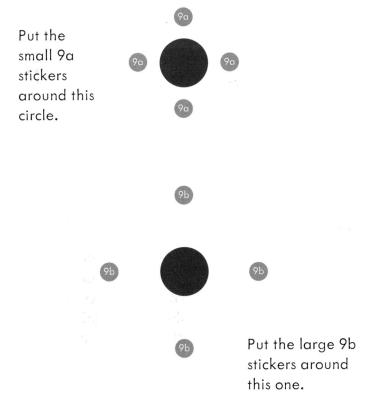

Put the large 9b stickers around this one.

# Crazy colours

With these two illusions you're going to make colours change as if by magic.

## SURPRISING SNAKES

Find the 10a stickers and check that they're the same colour. Stick half of them onto the orange snake and half onto the green one.

Do the stickers seem to be different shades of orange now? Try the same thing with the 10b stickers, on the yellow and blue snakes.

Stick the orange diamonds on these snakes.

Stick the blue diamonds on these snakes.

# WEIRD WAVES

Find the wave stickers for this page. Have a good look at them to make sure they're exactly the same colour.

Now stick one over each of the white strips on the picture. It's hard to believe they're still the same colour, isn't it?

# Impossible dot-to-dots

On these pages you're going to draw a series of weird 3-D shapes. They may look normal at first, but each one would be impossible to build.

## IMPOSSIBLE FORK

Using a thick black pen and a ruler, join the yellow dots and then the blue ones. This will create the well-known "fork" illusion.

Can you see why the shape is impossible?

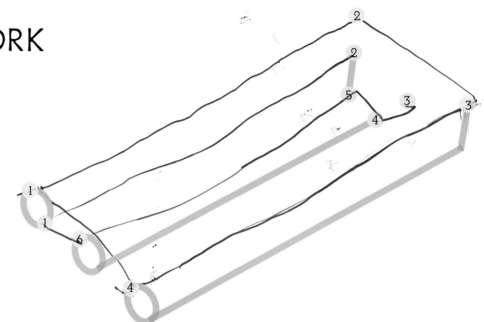

## IMPOSSIBLE CRATE

This box doesn't seem strange at first – but it will once you've joined the dots.

This triangle is another well-known impossible shape.

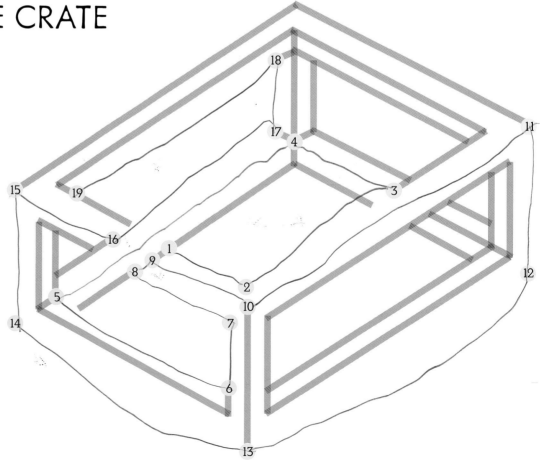

# IMPOSSIBLE STAIRCASE

Join these dots to make a staircase you would never find in real life. Can you see what's strange about it?

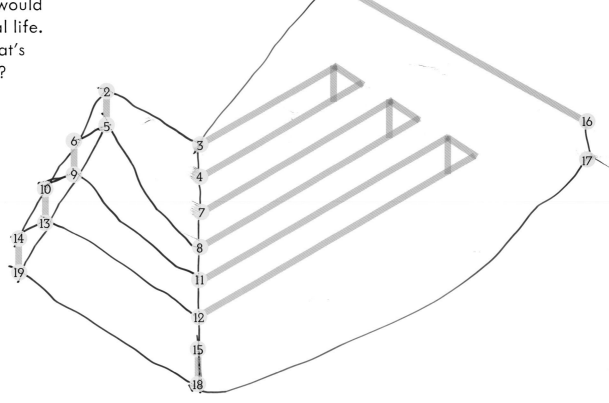

# IMPOSSIBLE OVERLAP

Here you're going to draw two perfectly normal shapes – but, as you'll see, they overlap in an impossible way.

Here's another 3-D shape illusion. Can you see why this arrangement of cubes is impossible?

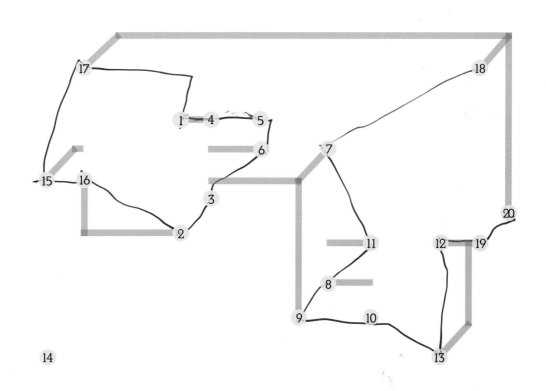

# Ghostly pictures

When you stare at anything for a long time, your eyes "remember" it and for a while afterwards you'll still see it. This is called an "after image", and on these pages you're going to explore how it works.

## AFTER IMAGES

This circle may look empty at the moment. But you're going to make lots of different pictures appear inside it, then vanish again. See the opposite page for how to do it.

Make sure you don't draw in this circle.

Colour this ghost black, leaving the eyes white. Stare at the cross in the middle for 30 seconds, then look inside the circle. What do you see?

Colour this sun dark blue. Now stare at the centre for 30 seconds as you did for the ghost. What colour is the sun when it appears inside the circle?

Colour this heart green, and repeat the same experiment. The heart won't be green anymore when it appears inside the circle. What colour is it?

Draw your own picture in this square. Make it a fairly simple shape, and use only one strong colour. Then try the same thing. Can you see the "ghost" of your picture?

# Bewildering spinners

On this page you're going to bamboozle your eyes with a set of spinning wheels. Each one creates a different amazing effect.

1. Find the stickers for this page. Stick the four wheels on a sheet of paper, and carefully cut them out.

2. Using a drawing pin, make a hole in the middle of each one. Push a cocktail stick halfway through it.

3. Rest one stick inside one end of a straw. Now spin the wheel as fast as you can, and stare at the image.

## WHAT HAPPENS?

Try spinning each of the four wheels. If you don't see an illusion straight away, don't give up. Keep spinning the wheel really fast and keep staring! Here's what should happen:

This wheel is black and white, but when you spin it you'll see colours appearing.

Spin this wheel clockwise. Does it seem to go round in the opposite direction?

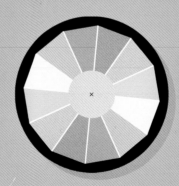

This wheel is full of different colours, but when you spin it they fade away.

Stare at this spinning wheel for 30 seconds, then look at your palm. What do you see?

# Imaginary shapes

Sometimes you see not what's really there, but what you assume must be there. Like the illusory shapes on this page, some of what you see only exists in your mind.

Find the stickers for this page, and add them where shown below. Make sure the edges of each sticker just cover the coloured lines on the page.

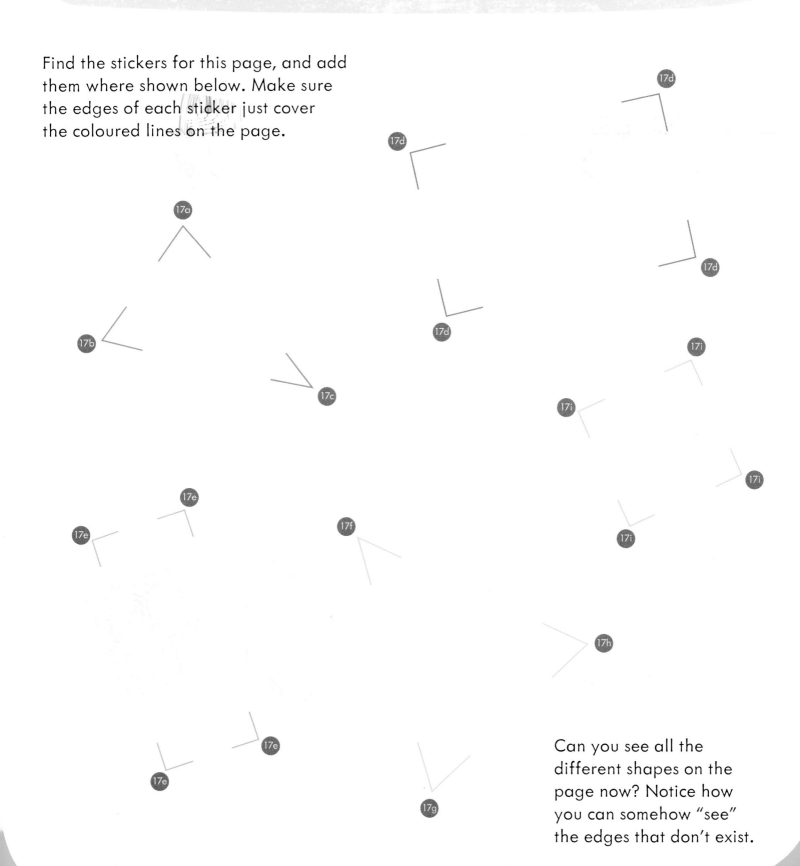

Can you see all the different shapes on the page now? Notice how you can somehow "see" the edges that don't exist.

# Can you follow the line?

It's surprising how easy it is to confuse your eyes. As you'll discover here, all you have to do is remove part of a line.

## SINGLE LINES?

Look at the broken orange stripe below. The two ends don't look as though they line up. But in fact they do – check with a ruler.

Use a ruler and a thick black pen to draw a broken line between each set of dots. Do the ends of your lines seem not to line up?

Make sure you leave a gap between the two black lines.

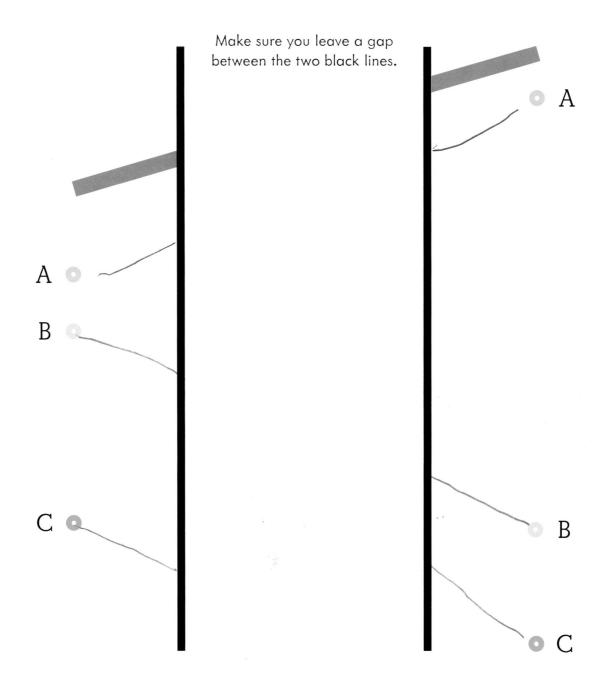

# BROKEN SHAPES

These two shapes are perfectly regular – they just have a section missing. Using a ruler, join the pairs of dots. Do the two parts of each shape look as if they don't quite line up anymore?

A ●      ● A

B ●      ● B

C ●    ● D

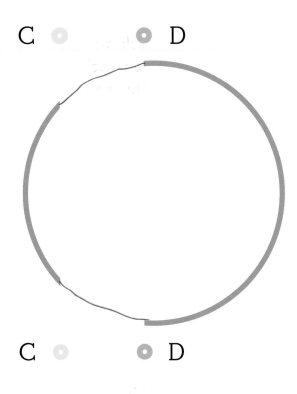

C ●    ● D

Try creating your own illusions using this idea – you could start by drawing a line with a pencil and a ruler, then rubbing out the middle section of the line.

# GUESS THE LINE

Use a ruler and a thin black pen to draw four lines, linking each pair of coloured dots. Now try to guess which one lines up with the orange line. Check your answer with a ruler – it's probably not the one you think!

# Colour confusion

You're going to fill this underwater scene with sharks and fish – and create an amazing colour illusion.

Find the 20a and 20b stickers. As you can see, the whole of each shark is the same colour. Stick them onto the picture, using the outlines as a guide. Do their heads look different from their tails now?

Look at the 20c stickers, which are also the same colour. Add some fish on the extreme left and some on the extreme right of the picture. As you know, they're all the same. But do they look the same now?

# Baffling buildings

In this extraordinary illusion, you're going to see how two areas that are identical in size and shape can be made to look very different.

Find stickers 21a and 21b. Before you remove them, use a ruler to check that they're exactly the same size and shape.

Now add them to the roofs of the buildings, as marked. Can you believe that they're the same? You might need to measure again to make sure!

Now add stickers 21c and 21d. They're identical too, but do they look it?

# Distorted shapes

Is it possible to make normal shapes appear bent and tilted simply by drawing a few straight lines?
You're about to find out.

## CONFUSING LINES

Use a ruler and a thick black pen to join point A to each dot on the right. What happens to the square?

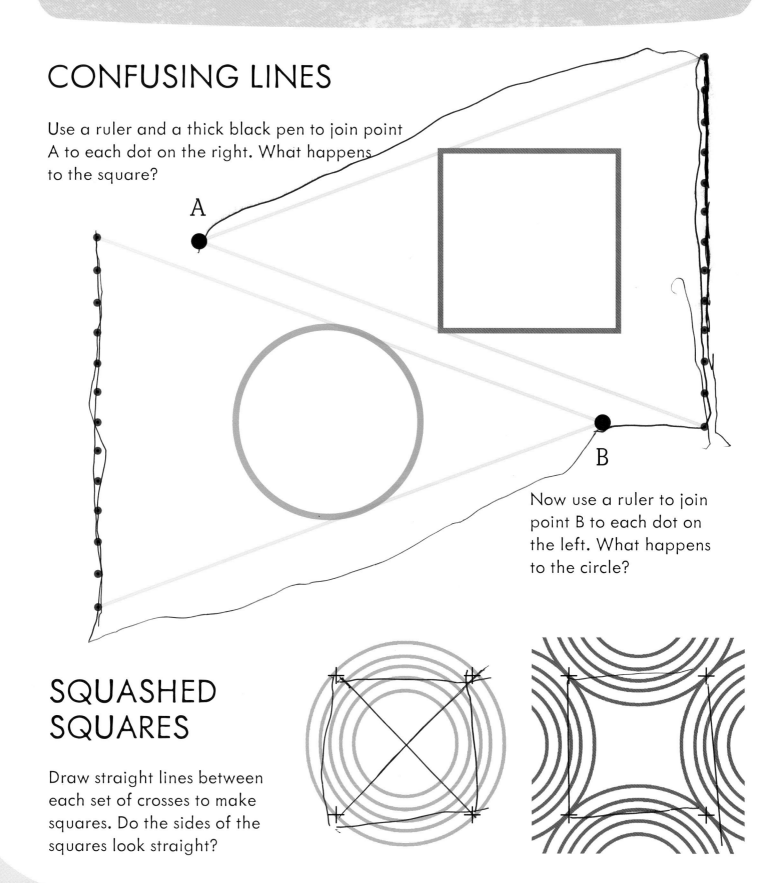

Now use a ruler to join point B to each dot on the left. What happens to the circle?

## SQUASHED SQUARES

Draw straight lines between each set of crosses to make squares. Do the sides of the squares look straight?

# TILTING RECTANGLES

Using a ruler and a thick black pen, carefully join each set of coloured dots to make four more rectangles.

You've drawn a set of perfect rectangles – all the sides are parallel. But look at your lines... do they seem to be tilting?

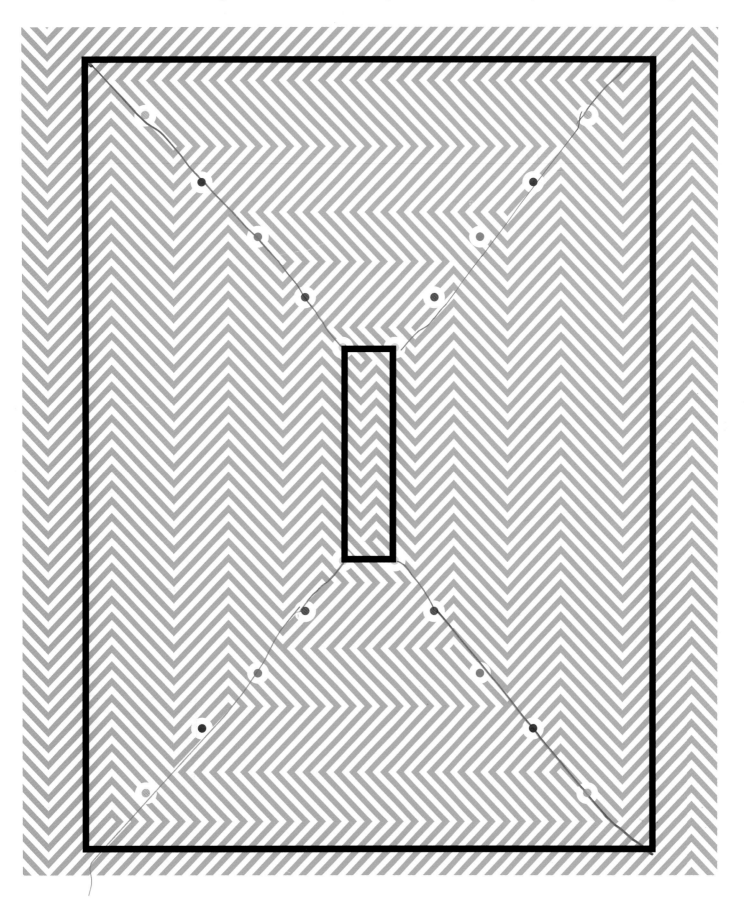

# Moving pictures

On these two pages you'll find out how you can fool your eyes so that pictures seem to float across the page, come to life, and even disappear completely.

## FLOATING IMAGES

Stare at this picture, and relax your eyes so that it starts to blur. Can you make it move until the fish ends up in the shark's mouth?

Finish drawing the web on the left. Then relax your eyes again – can you put the spider on the web?

Draw your own "floating image" in this box. It could be any two things that go together – a rocket on one side with the moon on the other, or a car and a garage, or whatever you can think of.

# VANISHING MONSTERS

Close your left eye and stare at the left-hand monster. Move the page closer to your eyes. Eventually the other monster will vanish... but not the yellow square it's in! Now stare at the right-hand monster and close your right eye. Can you make the other one vanish?

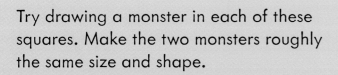

Try drawing a monster in each of these squares. Make the two monsters roughly the same size and shape.

Now do the same thing you did with the ones above, closing one eye at a time – can you make each one vanish?

# MONSTER MOVIE

Here's how to make a mini-movie with nothing more than a few stickers.

1. Find the stickers for this page. Stick the first one (25a) in the top corner of page 5 of this book.

2. Stick the next one on page 7, in the same place, then the next one on page 9, and so on.

3. Flick through the pages quickly, keeping your eyes on the monster. Can you see him dancing?

# Magic circle

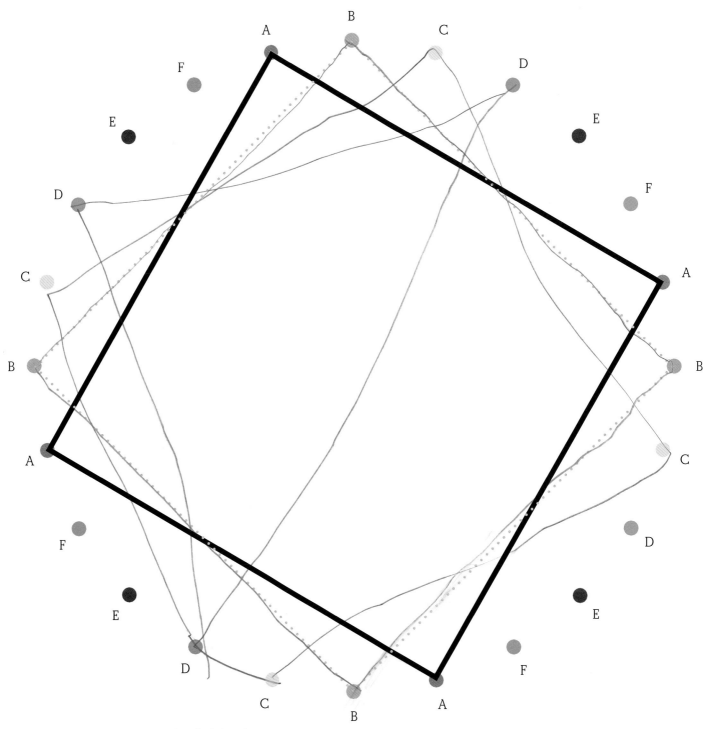

Using a ruler and a thick black
pen, connect all four B dots to make
a square, then connect each group
of dots to make lots more squares.

Now what do you
see in the middle?

# Squashed shapes

## STRANGE SQUARES

These three shapes are perfect squares.

Using a thick black pen, complete the pattern of slanting lines on each one. Make sure your lines are slanting in the correct direction.

Now move your eyes around the squares. Do they still look regular?

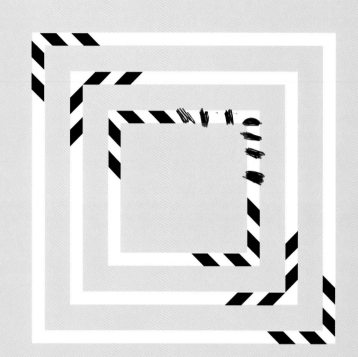

## QUIRKY CIRCLES

Now you're going to "squash" these perfect circles. Find sticker 27a and add it over the top. Does the outer circle look slightly squashed now? Add sticker 27b on top, and finally sticker 27c.

The circles are still perfectly round. But they don't look it, do they?

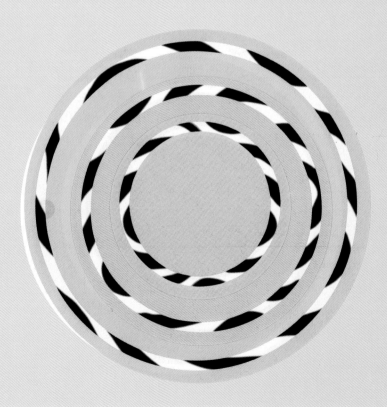

# Endless patterns

The patterns you're going to create here can be seen in two completely different ways. No matter how much you stare, you won't be able to decide what you're looking at.

## FOREGROUND OR BACKGROUND?

Colour all the arrows pointing to the right blue, and the ones pointing to the left red.

Does your picture show blue arrows with a red background, or exactly the opposite?

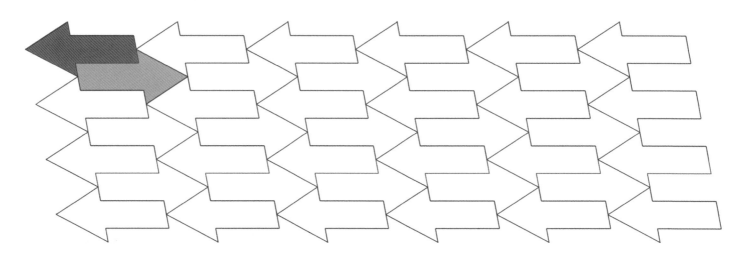

## LEFT OR RIGHT?

Do the same with this pattern, choosing two different colours for the fish.

Now take a look – are the fish swimming to the left or the right? It's both!

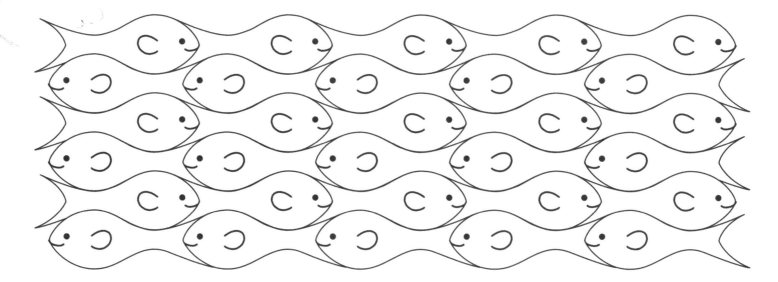

# 3-D CUBES

Look at the two cubes on the right. One is yellow at the bottom, and the other yellow on top. Now look at the shape next to them – it contains both cubes, and your eyes will "flip" between the two.

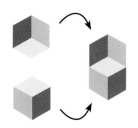

Complete the colouring on the cubes below, following the same pattern. Can you see how the whole group of cubes can be viewed in two different ways?

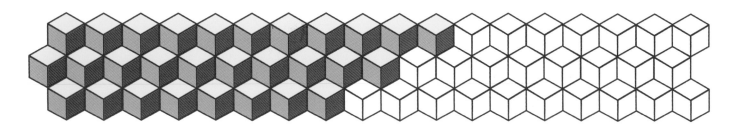

Now create the same illusion by drawing more of these larger cubes, using the graph paper to help you. Choose any three colours for the different faces of the cubes.

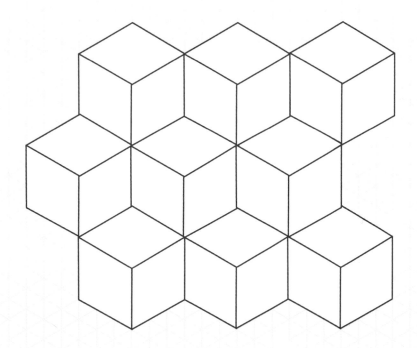

Count the triangles to help you draw the cubes.

# Which way?

Faces are something you see every day, so they shouldn't be able to fool your eyes. But these ones will.

## TOPSY-TURVY FACES

Look at this face. Now turn the book upside down. What do you see?

Using the first face as an example, can you draw hair, eyes, noses, beards and glasses on the other faces to make them work upside down too?

## MYSTERIOUS EYES

Find the stickers for this page. As you can see, they're identical – both pairs of eyes are the same. Now stick them above the two noses. Are they still looking the same way?

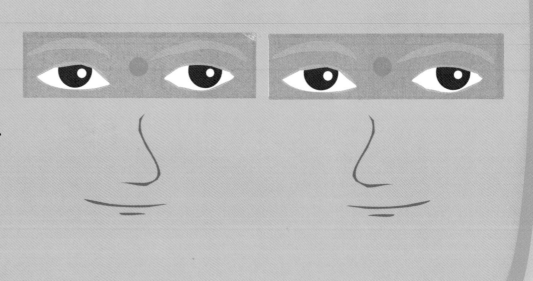

# Catch the bird

On this page you're going to create a fun illusion where you draw two separate pictures and watch them become one.

Make the cage a bit bigger than the bird.

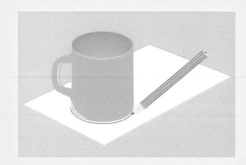

1. Make a circle on a piece of thin white card, by drawing around a mug. Then cut it out.

2. Draw a bird on one side of the circle and a cage on the other – but make the cage upside down.

3. Make two small holes on each side of the card. Cut two pieces of string as long as your arm.

4. Thread string through one pair of holes and knot the ends. Do the same on the other side.

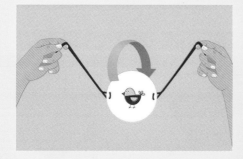

5. Hold the knots so that the circle hangs down. Flip the circle over and around until the string is twisted tightly.

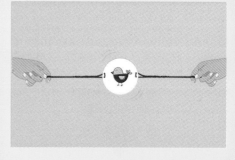

6. Now, with both hands, pull the string tight. The circle will spin really fast. What do you see?

## WHAT'S HAPPENING?

When you spin the circle, your eyes see the bird and the cage one after another... but so quickly that they seem to become one.

# Illusion puzzles

See how much you've discovered about illusions by trying the questions below. Be careful – the most obvious answer is often wrong. (The correct answers are at the bottom.)

1. Which of the inner circles on the right is exactly the same colour as the one on the left?

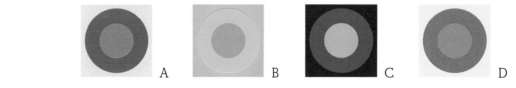

2. Which of the lines on the right is exactly the same length as the one on the left?

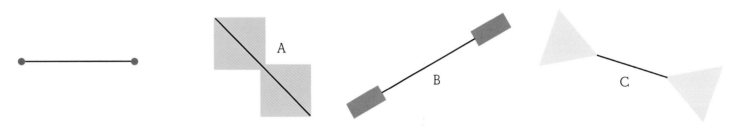

3. Which orange hexagon is the largest?

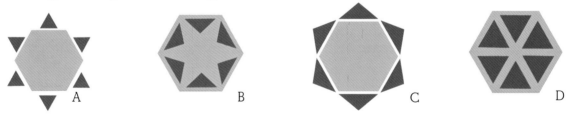

4. Which one of these blue shapes is a perfect square?

5. Look at the three crosses. Which one is exactly halfway up the triangle?

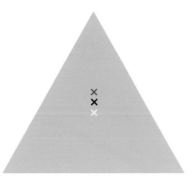

Answers: 1. Surprisingly, it's circle C, even though it seems much paler. The frames around the circles influence your perception of the colours. 2. Line B is the answer, but the different shapes around the lines make this hard to see. 3. Did you think it was C? Actually both B and D are bigger. The largest of all is D. 4. The only perfect square is B. 5. It's the red cross – but most people think it's the black one, or even the yellow one.

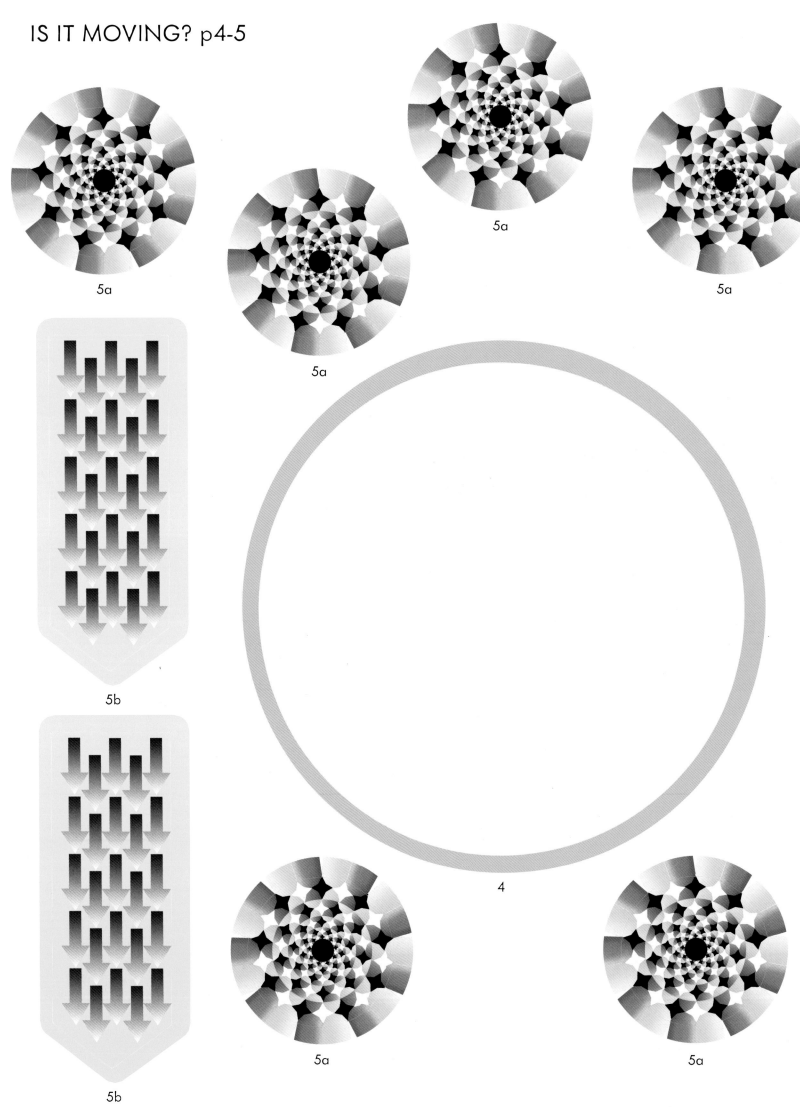

5a

5a

5a

5a

5b

5b

4

5a

5a

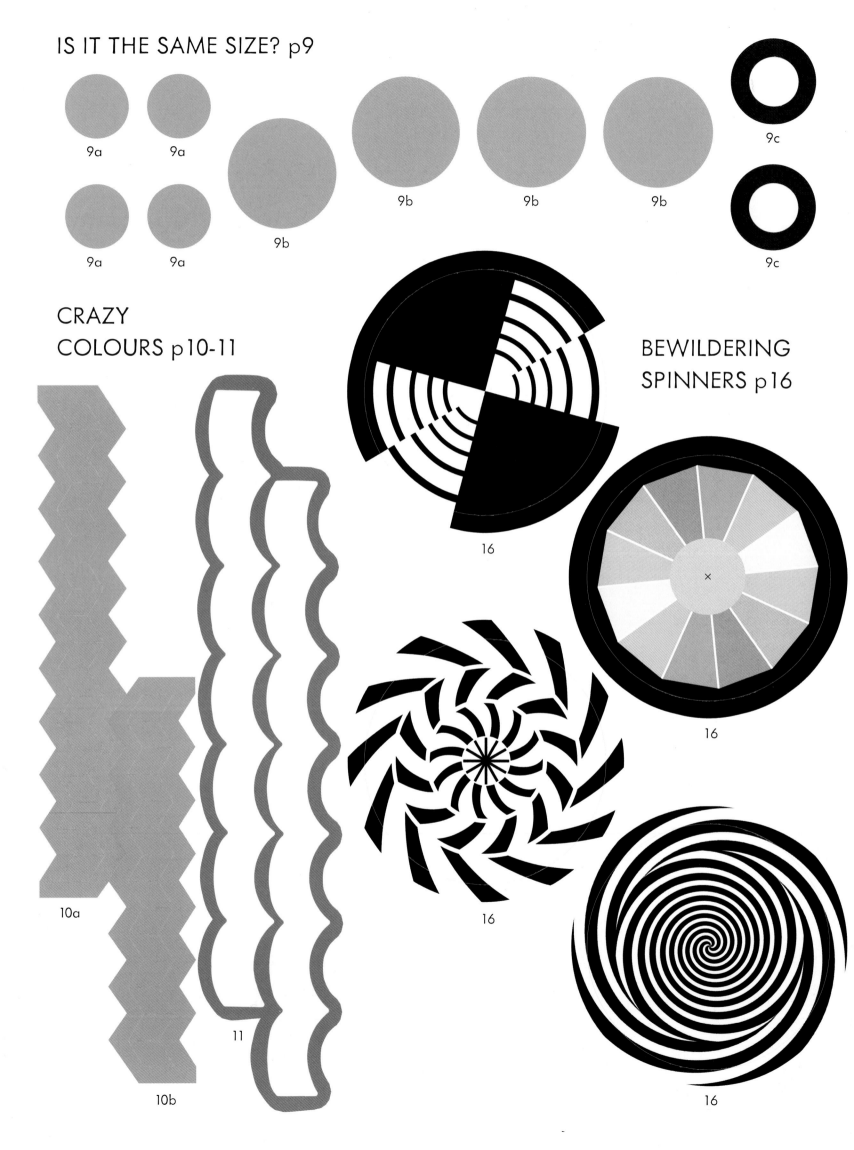

IS IT THE SAME SIZE? p9

9a  9a

9a  9a

9b

9b

9b

9b

9c

9c

CRAZY
COLOURS p10-11

10a

11

10b

BEWILDERING
SPINNERS p16

16

16

16

16

# IMAGINARY SHAPES p17

17a 17b 17c

17i 17i 17i

17e 17e 17i

17e 17e

17f 17g 17h

17d 17d 17d 17d

# COLOUR CONFUSION p20

20a 20c
20c

20c

20c

20c

20b

20c 20c

# BAFFLING BUILDINGS p21

21c 21a

21d 21b

# MOVING PICTURES p25

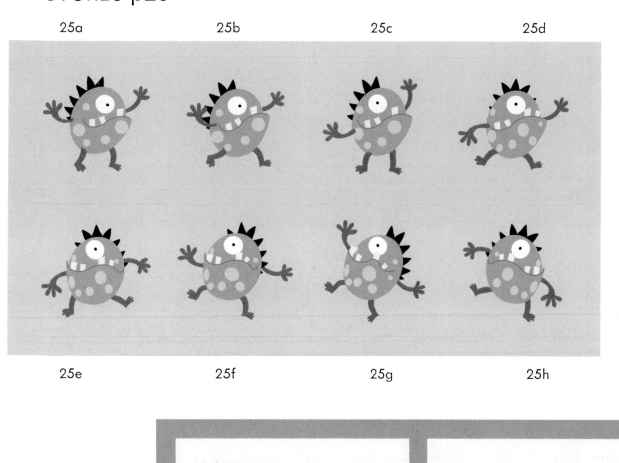

25a  25b  25c  25d

25e  25f  25g  25h

## WHICH WAY? p30

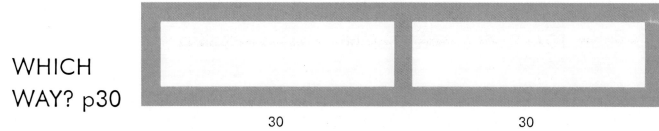

30  30

## SQUASHED SHAPES p27

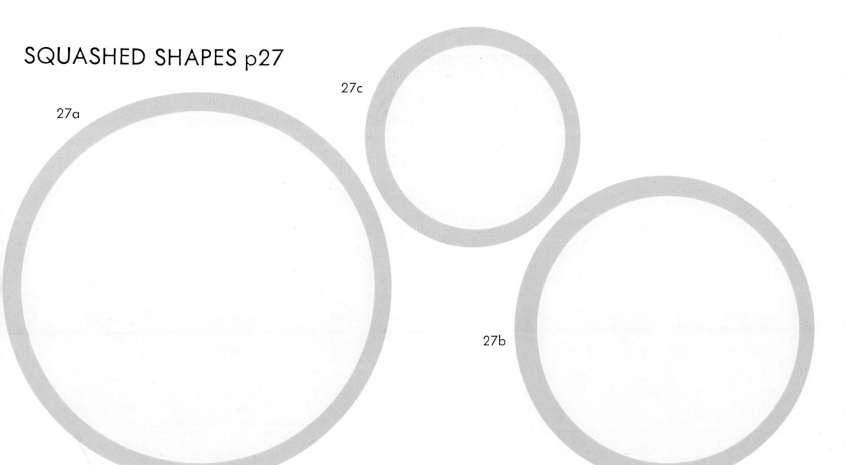

27a  27c  27b